By **Sam Watkins** Illustrated by **David O'Connell**

CREATURE TEACHER

Out to Win

STONE ARCH BOOKS
a capstone imprint

For Isaac, already a football legend — S.W.
For Lizzie, Sarah, and all the brilliant
team at OUP — D.O'C.

Creature Teacher Out to Win is published by Stone Arch Books,
A Capstone Imprint
1710 Roe Crest Drive
North Mankato, Minnesota 56003
www.mycapstone.com

Text copyright © Sam Watkins 2015
Illustrations copyright © David O'Connell 2015
Published in American English in 2018 by Stone Arch Books

Creature Teacher Out to Win was originally published in English in 2015. This
translation is published by arrangement with Oxford University Press.

Library of Congress Cataloging-in-Publication Data is available
on the Library of Congress website.

ISBN: 978-1-4965-5704-9 (Library Binding)
ISBN: 978-1-4965-5687-5 (Paperback)
ISBN: 978-1-4965-5708-7 (eBook PDF)

Summary:
Something's out of control in the classroom! When Jake's teacher, Mr. Hyde, turns into
the naughty Creature at a soccer tournament, how on earth are he and his friends going
to keep Mr. Hyde's secret? Chaos is bound to happen when Creature's around!

Designer:
Mackenzie Lopez

Printed in Canada.
010407F17

TABLE OF CONTENTS

CHAPTER 1

BANANAS LOSE APPEAL FOR BARNABY

"What on EARTH is Barnaby wearing?" Jake said to Alexis.

Barnaby, their classmate, was standing near the gate to Bembley Road Sports Club, wearing a strange yellow and black outfit that went over his head, ending in a pointy hood. Underneath, he had a face like he'd just eaten a large mouthful of moldy cabbage soup.

"Dunno," Alexis said, giggling. "He's not happy about it, though."

As they reached Barnaby, Jake realized it was a banana costume.

"If you laugh, I'll never speak to you again," Barnaby growled. "Ever."

Jake kept in a laugh. "OK, I won't — but why are you dressed as a banana?"

Barnaby pointed. *"That's* why."

Not far off, Jake saw a stand with a sign which read:

BURT'S BANANA SMOOTHIES

Sponsors of the County
Junior League Soccer Tournament

"That company has put loads of money into the tournament," said Barnaby bitterly. "So Mrs. Blunt decided it would be great to have all the student council members dress up as bananas, to promote them. Our principal's evilness knows no bounds!"

"Oh, so Mrs. Blunt made you a council member, then?" asked Jake.

"No, I volunteered. But I didn't know I'd have to wear a stupid fruit costume," said the angry banana.

Alexis couldn't keep a straight face any longer. "Ha, ha! Oh, Barnaby, that's such bad luck! I'd never be seen dead in a banana costume."

A mean laugh from behind Jake made him turn around. Amelia Trotter-Hogg, ponytailed pest of Class 5A, was standing there, a look of evil happiness on her face.

"For once, I agree with Alexis," Amelia said, smirking. She turned to Barnaby. "I thought this was a soccer tournament, not a fruit and veggie competition."

"What are you doing here?" said Barnaby coldly. "I thought you had Prissypants' Pony Club on Saturdays." Barnaby shook his banana-head as if flipping a ponytail.

Amelia glared. "It's *Priscilla's* Pony Club, actually." She turned to go, then looked back. "And you'll find out why I'm here soon enough . . ."

She marched off. Barnaby glared after her.

"It's her fault I'm dressed like this! I'd have been on the team with you guys if she hadn't told on me."

"You can't blame Amelia," Alexis said. "You're the one who put slugs in her lunch box. You should have known it would get you a day's work on the Rockery — it was just bad luck that was the day they picked the team."

A day's work on the Rockery was the punishment for any student getting three Sad Faces. A Sad Face was given for breaking a school rule. There were a hundred and forty-one (or maybe two) school rules, so it was quite easy to break one without even knowing you had, and Barnaby found it easier than most.

"Jake! Alexis!"

Woodstock was walking toward them, with a little old man dressed from head to toe in soccer gear. The old man's face was

painted in blue and white stripes, their team colors, and he was wearing a ball-tipped hat to match. He held a megaphone to his mouth.

"WE'RE ON OUR WAY TO BEMBLEY, WE'RE GONNA MISS ASSEMBLY, DA DAAA DAAA DA! DA DAAA DAAA DA!"

Woodstock rolled his eyes.

"Stop it, Granddad!" He turned to the others. "My granddad's crazy about soccer. In fact, he's just plain crazy. Granddad, these are my friends."

"SPEAK UP, BOY!" Granddad bellowed into the megaphone. Jake's eardrums shook in pain.

"I said — these are my friends, Jake and Alexis!" Woodstock yelled in his ear.

"No need to shout," Granddad said. "I'm not deaf."

Granddad shook Jake's and Alexis's hands, then turned to Barnaby.

"And who's this?"

"Oh — hi, Barnaby," Woodstock said, recognizing Barnaby for the first time. "Sorry, I didn't recognize you in that costume. Granddad, this is Barnaby . . ."

"Hello, Bananaby," Granddad said.

Alexis almost giggled. Barnaby's face turned more cherry- than banana-colored.

"BAR-NA-BY!" shouted Woodstock. "Oh, never mind. Barnaby, can you help my granddad find a seat? We have to go and get changed now."

Barnaby sighed as Granddad took his arm, chatting away merrily. "Thank you, Bananaby. Unusual name. Is it Scandinavian?"

He dragged Barnaby off into the crowd.

Jake shook his head. "Poor Bananaby — I mean Barnaby."

Woodstock chuckled. "Leave it to Granddad to come up with that one! Yeah, Barnaby really wanted to be on the team, didn't he?"

"Look, never mind him," Alexis said. "What's important is that we win the Golden Ball trophy. We did well in the first rounds and have been practicing extra hard. As Mr. Hyde always says: what are we?"

"Winners!" Jake and Woodstock cheered, but a sudden pang of worry hit Jake at the mention of their teacher. Everyone knew that Mr. Hyde was the best teacher in the universe. *Not* everyone knew that Mr. Hyde had an unfortunate habit of turning into a very naughty and chaos-creating creature when he got stressed or over-excited.

"Let's hope Mr. Hyde doesn't turn into Creature today," he said. "We won't be winners then — we'll just be in trouble!"

"We'll help keep him as calm as possible," said Alexis. "He said he'd sort out our jerseys and take them to the locker room."

"Let's go then," Woodstock said. "The first game starts in about twenty minutes."

On their way, Jake had a nagging feeling that something was wrong. Then he remembered what Amelia had said. "You'll find out why I'm here in a bit." *What had she meant by that?*

"Uh oh. What's this?" Woodstock pointed as they approached the locker room.

Jake saw a small crowd of people. Their two classmates, Nora and Karl, were there. Facing them was the ponytailed pest, Amelia Trotter-Hogg.

Even worse luck, next to Amelia stood Mrs. Blunt. Mrs. Blunt was dressed in a very sharp suit and huge sunglasses. She was leaning toward Nora and Karl like a praying mantis about to strike.

CHAPTER 2

JERSEY CATASTROPHE CAUSES CHAOS!

Jake, Alexis, and Woodstock ran up beside Nora.

"What's happening?" Jake asked her in a low voice. "Why is Amelia here?"

"Amelia is playing on our team now," Nora said through gritted teeth.

"What? Why?" Alexis demanded.

Mrs. Blunt leaned forward. "Rona was injured in a game yesterday and is unable to play today. So I have decided to put Amelia on the team in her place."

"But that's ridiculous!" Alexis cried. "One of the substitutes should play! Ralph or Oliver. They've been to all the practices. Amelia hasn't been to a single one!"

"We've got a flawless game plan," Nora added, tapping her clipboard importantly. "Any change in line-up is going to cause major problems."

Amelia squinted at the clipboard."What are all those numbers and scribbles? That's

math, not soccer! Stick to what you're good at, boring Nor—" She shot a glance at Mrs. Blunt and stopped.

Nora looked as though she was about to whack Amelia with the flawless game plan. Karl and Jake grabbed her.

"Don't, Nora," Jake muttered.

Mrs. Blunt's mouth twisted into what Jake imagined she thought was a smile, but looked more like a shark getting ready to bite your legs off.

"So, it's settled. Amelia will replace Rona as vice-captain," Mrs. Blunt said. "Now, if you'll excuse me, I have more important things to attend to."

She stomped away.

Alexis, Nora, Karl, Jake, and Woodstock looked at each other, then at Amelia.

Amelia gave them an overjoyed smirk.

Alexis's face went purple with rage. "I'm team captain, and I'm not —"

"Helloooo! What's going on?"

Jake looked up to see Mr. Hyde bouncing toward them. He was wearing a blue tracksuit, bright orange shoes, and a sweatband that made his hair stick up like a startled porcupine. Over his shoulder hung a large bag.

Alexis ran to him. "Sir, Mrs. Blunt says Amelia has to play in Rona's place. It'll mess everything up!"

Mr. Hyde scratched his head. He looked at Amelia, who suddenly managed to look sorry for herself.

"Come now," Mr. Hyde said. "One banana does not a fruit salad make."

Everyone looked blank.

"Sorry, sir?" Jake asked, confused.

He had a sudden shock of fear that his teacher was changing into Creature. Mr. Hyde sometimes said odd things just before he changed. Jake glanced at his teacher, but Mr. Hyde looked calm and not at all like he was about to disappear in a puff of smoke.

"Bananas aren't great in fruit salad," said Nora. "They go all brown and slimy."

"Forget the fruit salad thing," Mr. Hyde said quickly. "I meant that it doesn't matter *who's* on the team, it's about everyone *working together* as a team. Alexis, as captain, it's your job to make sure they do that."

Just then, a crackle came over a loudspeaker.

"TEN MINUTES TO KICK-OFF! ALL TEAMS TO THEIR FIELDS, PLEASE!"

Alexis gasped. "We're not even changed yet! Sir, have you got the jerseys?"

Mr. Hyde hoisted the bag off his shoulder and unzipped it. Inside was a stack of brand new jerseys, each in a clear plastic wrapper. He handed each player a jersey. Alexis and Amelia disappeared into the girls' changing room; Jake, Karl, and Woodstock went into the boys'.

Jake tore the wrapper off his jersey and pulled the shirt over his head. Woodstock and Karl did the same.

They looked at each other.

"What's happened to our jerseys?" Woodstock exclaimed.

Jake looked down at himself. His shirt was shiny and new, and white and blue . . . and came down to his knees!

No one spoke. Then Jake heard a muffled shriek from next door. They all ran back into the locker room at the same time as

Alexis and Amelia burst out of the other door. Their shirts, too, looked more like big, baggy dresses. They all stared at each other.

"These are adult jerseys!" Alexis cried.

"Clever Mr. Hyde must have picked up the wrong ones," Amelia growled.

Jake held up his shorts. They were so huge his whole body would fit into one leg.

"We can't play in these —" he began. At that moment, a voice boomed out from a speaker on the wall.

"FIVE MINUTES TO KICK-OFF. ALL PLAYERS REPORT TO THEIR FIELDS IMMEDIATELY."

Karl groaned. "Now what?"

Alexis took a deep breath. "We'll have to wear them for this game. We've got to compete in matching jerseys — they won't let us play otherwise."

Everyone trooped back into their respective changing rooms. Jake managed to tie his tent-like shorts on, but they were very loose. He waddled back outside just as Alexis's head poked around the girls' changing room door.

"You guys go on ahead! I'll meet you there in a sec. I need to go to the bathroom!"

"Yeah, me too," Jake heard Amelia say.

The boys ran out of the locker room and dodged through the crowd to the fields, shirts billowing out behind them like parachutes.

"Where's our field?" puffed Karl. Jake peered around, then he saw Mr. Hyde standing with a referee, waving at them frantically from beside one of the fields.

"Here they are," said Mr. Hyde as they ran up. He stared at Jake in surprise.

"Why are you wearing long dresses?"

"They're extra-large adult jerseys, sir," Jake panted. "You must have bought the wrong ones."

Mr. Hyde slapped his forehead. "Oh no! I was in such a hurry this morning. I'll call

the shop and get someone to bring ones that
will fit."

He turned to the referee. "Can they play
in their normal clothes for now?"

The referee shook his head sternly.
"Teams must be in matching jerseys."

Mr. Hyde dropped his head, disappointed.

The referee turned to Jake, and asked, "Where's the rest of your team?"

Jake looked back toward the locker room. He could see Amelia making her way toward them, but, strangely, Alexis was nowhere in sight.

"Where's Alexis?" Jake asked, as Amelia walked up. "The game's about to start!"

Amelia shrugged. "I don't know. She went to the bathroom, then disappeared. She must have chickened out and run off!"

CHAPTER 3

TEAM RALLIES AFTER COLOSSAL SHORTS CONFUSION

Everyone gaped at Amelia.

Nora snorted. "Yeah right! Alexis would never miss a soccer game."

"We have to find her!" Woodstock exclaimed.

The referee shook his head. "No time. We've got to start the game."

He marched onto the field, followed by the other team who stared at Jake's team in their huge, baggy jerseys and nudged each other, giggling.

Amelia glared at them.

"What are you staring at?" she snapped. "Never seen real talent before? OK, team, follow me."

"You can't tell us what to do," Karl said.

Amelia smirked. "Actually, I can. Mrs. Blunt made me vice-captain, so now that Alexis isn't here, *I'm* captain."

It was true. There was nothing Jake and the rest of the team could do except follow after Amelia.

"HEY! WAIT!" an urgent voice called.

Jake turned. "Alexis!"

Alexis was racing toward them, her shirt flapping wildly.

"What happened to you?!" Jake asked, relieved, as she skidded up.

"The bathroom door was stuck," Alexis panted. "It must have jammed. I called and called, but everyone had gone! I had to climb out of the window."

"Captains, please!" called the ref. With a sour face, Amelia stepped back to let Alexis take her place for the coin toss, then everyone ran to their positions.

Jake was playing defense, with Amelia. As he took his position, he saw Mr. Hyde, Nora, and Woodstock's granddad standing at the side of the field. Mr. Hyde was talking on a cellphone and looking a bit stressed.

The whistle blew.

Pheeeeeeeeeeeeeeeep!

Game on!

The captain of the other team passed the ball toward a player near Jake. Jake tried to get a toe on it, but his shorts slipped down, catching his foot and sending him flying. Scrambling up, he saw the player dribbling the ball toward their goal, where Karl was crouched down, ready — but where was Amelia?!

"SMILE, DARLING!"

Jake's mouth dropped. He saw Amelia striking a pose for her mom, who was by the sideline, taking a photograph.

What is she doing?! Jake panicked.

Amelia wasn't paying attention to the game and didn't even notice the other team's striker dribble the ball right past her. He kicked it at the goal.

Karl prepared to dive for it, and, as he did so, his shorts fell down. Flushing, he bent to pull them up, and the ball whizzed over his head to the back of the net.

"GOAL!" whooped the goal-scorer, amidst cheers from the crowd. Jake ran over to Amelia.

"AMELIA! What were you doing?"

She tossed her head. "I wasn't doing anything!"

"Exactly —" Jake began, but the ref was waving them back to positions.

Pheeeeeeeeeeeeeep!

Still furious with Amelia, Jake kept his eye on her but this made him miss a couple of easy tackles. *Focus on the ball,* Jake told himself firmly, hitching up his shorts for the umpteenth time. He saw the ball whiz toward their goal again and raced after it, but just as he was nearly to it, Alexis appeared out of nowhere and whisked the ball away. She flew back up the left side of the field, shirt billowing, dodging defenders.

"Over here!" Woodstock yelled from center field, but Alexis ignored him and took the shot.

Jake shook his head. It was going wide. But wait! Woodstock was there, scuffling toward the airborne ball, trying desperately to hold his shorts up! But it was no good. They were going . . . going . . . gone!

The shorts dropped to his ankles, tripping him forward, and, as he fell, his head whacked the ball into the net, catching the goalie completely by surprise. Woodstock looked up from the ground, rubbing his head.

"W-what happened?" he asked, dazed.

"GOOOOOOOOOAL!" Jake bellowed, racing down the field to leap on Woodstock.

"THERE'S ONLY ONE WOODSTOCK STONE!" yelled Woodstock's granddad. He fell off his chair in excitement.

As the whistle blew for half-time, Alexis called everyone together.

"We've got to keep the pressure on," she said. "Pass the ball to me whenever you can."

Nora frowned. "It's about teamwork, Alexis."

"Whatever. I mean, yes, of course. Come on team, I — I mean, we — can do this!"

As the second half got underway Jake tried to do as Alexis had asked, but the other team were marking her closely. No one could get the ball near her. With five minutes to go Jake saw his chance. He dodged a defender just outside the box and looked around for Alexis.

"Take the shot, Jake!" shouted Nora. "A thirty-degree angle should do it!"

Taking a deep breath, Jake fired, watching the ball sail toward the net almost as if in slow motion.

THWACK! Someone rammed into him from behind! As he flew forward, he caught a glimpse of the ball whizzing into the top corner of the goal, missing the goalie's fingertips by inches.

Then, *CRACK!* He hit the ground, his ankle twisting painfully under him.

Jake heard a roaring that could have been the crowd or his ears ringing. He rolled over, trying to catch his breath, pain stabbing through his ankle.

"Stretcher!" he heard someone shout.

Stretcher?! "No, I'm all right," Jake panted. He staggered dizzily to his feet.

"Are you sure?" Woodstock looked worried. Jake waved him away.

"I'm fine!" *There's no way I'm being carried off now!* he thought.

The last minutes of the game were a blur to Jake. As the final whistle blew, he heaved a sigh of relief. His ankle was throbbing badly, but it was worth it — they were through to the semi-finals!

Jake limped to meet the others as a storm of cheering burst from the crowd. Amelia ran back to her parents to pose for more photos. On the sideline, Woodstock's granddad was singing into his megaphone, while Nora shouted something in his ear. Next to them, Mr. Hyde was grinning like a Cheshire cat, waving a scarf over his head, and steaming.

Jake grinned and started to wave back.

Then Jake stopped.

Steaming? Jake squinted across the field at his teacher. Steam was rising from Mr. Hyde like he was a boiling kettle. And his face was a bright red.

"NOOOOO!" Jake gasped.

FAAAAAAAAAAAAARRRRRT!

Wheeeeeeee · · · · · · · · · ·

POP! POP! POP!

BANG!

CHAPTER 4

CREATURE CAUSES
QUARTER-FINAL CHAOS!

A super-loud fart noise ripped through the air. Screaming people flung themselves to the ground as a cloud of purple smoke engulfed them. As the smoke began to clear, Jake saw that the only person left upright was Woodstock's granddad. He peered at the people cowering around him on the ground, a puzzled look on his face.

"Granddad! I told him not to bring those smoke bombs!" Woodstock groaned.

"That was no smoke bomb!" Jake exclaimed. "That was Mr. Hyde changing into Creature!"

"Oh no!" Alexis took off toward the sideline, followed by Woodstock and Karl. Jake limped after them to where Mr. Hyde had been standing a few moments before. Woodstock's granddad peered at them as they approached.

"Oh, it's you, Woody. I think I just farted a real stinker," he said. "Must have been that prune juice I had this morning."

"Why do you drink that stuff? It always makes you gassy," Woodstock said, his eyes darting around, trying to spot Creature. Nora crawled out from under a chair, coughing and gasping for air.

"Mr. Hyde . . . Creature . . ." she managed to choke out.

Jake grabbed her. "Nora! Where did he go? Did you see?"

Catching her breath, Nora pointed. Through the clearing smoke, Jake saw a small, furry shape bouncing away. He was still wearing the sweatband around his head, making him look like a cross between a tennis player from the 1980s and a gorilla that had shrunk in the wash.

"After him!" Nora, Woodstock, Karl, and Alexis ran after Creature, with Jake limping painfully along behind. Jake saw Creature bounce over a man who was trying to get up off the ground, nearly knocking his hat off. The man gaped, then ducked as Alexis and the others all leapt over him too. He rubbed his eyes.

"Did you see that? Looked like some kind of monkey!" the man exclaimed as Jake hobbled up.

Jake thought quickly.

"Oh no, that's just our, um, team mascot," he said. "He got over-excited!"

"He's heading for the next field!" shouted Karl. "The game is still in play!"

Alexis put out an extra spurt of energy and hurled herself toward Creature as he reached the sideline. At that moment, two banana-clad student council members staggered in front of him, carrying between them a huge bag full of soccer balls. As Alexis sprang forward to grab him, Creature took a flying leap and landed slap-bang on top of the bag.

"JEEPER!" Creature squawked.

"Eeeeeeeeeeeeeeek!" cried the bananas.

They dropped the bag, which burst open, knocking Alexis back in a thundering avalanche of balls. Behind her, Karl and Woodstock tried to avoid the wave of balls rolling under their feet. Jake dodged the balls and made a lunge toward Creature.

"Ow!" Pain shot through Jake's ankle, and he stumbled to a halt. Creature bounced joyfully onto the field and headed for the goal, where a player was about to take a free kick. A line of opponent defenders stood in front of him, waiting for the whistle.

The ref sucked in his breath, ready to blow.

Creature bounced up to him and grabbed the whistle out of his mouth.

Pheeeeeeeeeeeeeeeep! Creature gave it a healthy blast, right in the astonished ref's face.

Facing the other way, the player taking the kick didn't see what had happened, but on the whistle, he ran up to the ball. Just

as he kicked it, Creature launched himself at the ball and wrapped himself around it. *THWACK!* The ball and Creature rocketed into the air and somersaulted over the line of defenders toward the goal . . .

"KIPPPPPPPPPERRRRRRRRRRRR!"

The goalie saw Creature spinning toward him like a spiraling firework and threw himself, cowering, to the ground. Jake watched, open-mouthed, as ball and Creature shot over the top of the net and landed — *SPLAT!* — in a large vat of ketchup on a hot dog stand. Creature's surprised head appeared over the side, almost entirely covered in ketchup.

"We can catch him now!" Karl cried to the others. They started making their way through the crowd of confused spectators along the sideline. Jake tried to keep up, but every step was agony, plus his shorts kept falling down. It was no good. He had to stop. Nora saw him and ran back.

"Jake? Are you OK?"

KETCHUP

He swallowed. "I, I'll be all right . . ."

Nora looked around. "Look, why don't we go to the cafeteria? It's just over there."

Jake looked anxiously after the others, but his ankle twinged again.

He grimaced. "OK, I will. But you should go help the others."

"No. I'm staying with you," she said.

Nora helped Jake across to the cafeteria. He sat down at a table and stared moodily out of the window while Nora went to fetch two banana smoothies. *This whole thing is my fault*, he thought. He should have kept a better eye on Mr. Hyde. And he shouldn't have got himself injured, because now he couldn't even help to catch Creature.

A loud voice made him turn.

"HURRY UP, GIRL!" Mrs. Blunt was standing behind Nora in the line of customers. She was with a man carrying a large camera — the reporter from the local paper, Jake realized.

Mrs. Blunt tapped angrily on the counter and snapped at the girl serving Nora.

"Let's go, I haven't got all day!"

Jake rolled his eyes. Whoever had taught Mrs. Blunt manners had not done a very good job!

Jake looked out of the window again, and noticed Amelia talking to one of the banana-clad council members. He handed her a big bag, and she disappeared off in the direction of the locker room. As the student council member turned his banana self around, Jake saw that it was Barnaby.

"What's going on out there?" Nora had come back with the smoothies.

"I think our real jerseys have —" Jake began, but at that moment, a door banged loudly behind him. Nora's eyes widened, and she nearly spat her smoothie out.

"Oh no!" she said. "Guess who's here . . ."

CHAPTER 5

PRINCIPAL SPLATTED IN MILKSHAKE SHOCKER!

Jake whirled around. In the doorway stood Creature, wild-eyed, and dripping globs of ketchup all over the floor. He looked like something out of a horror movie. People at the tables nearest him jumped up, open-mouthed in shock.

"What *is* it?" someone yelled.

Jake and Nora pushed their way through tables toward him.

"It's OK," Jake called, raising his hands for calm. "He's our team mascot!"

"He's covered in blood!" a woman near them said, hands over her mouth. "Someone should call an ambulance!"

"It's only ketchup," Nora said.

Creature saw Jake and Nora approaching and started to back out toward the door when it burst open again. Alexis ran in, Karl and Woodstock behind her.

"Squaaaaaaaark!"

Cornered, Creature's eyes darted around. He spotted a table where a couple was sitting. Without warning, he shot sideways and leapt onto it, landing with a crash in the woman's plate of French fries.

The woman threw herself backward, as fries flew in all directions.

"What the —" The man tried to grab him, but the now fry-covered Creature grabbed a fork and pole-vaulted himself onto the next table, crash-landing between two large chocolate ice creams. The two girls sitting at the table sprang up in fright, as Creature grabbed both ice creams, and tipped them noisily into his throat.

"Mmmmm!" He wiped a chocolate mustache from his lips.

"Grab him now," Jake whispered to Karl, who was closest to Creature.

Karl tiptoed up behind Creature, but Creature turned and saw him.

BUUUUUUUUUUUUUUURP!

A loud, chocolaty burp erupted from his open mouth.

"Ugh!" Karl jumped back, as Creature bounded off.

"Excuse us!" Jake skidded around the panicked girls after Creature. He was heading toward a corner table, slightly hidden behind a vending machine. When he saw who was sitting at the table, Jake skidded to a halt and jumped behind the machine.

"Mrs. Blunt!" he hissed.

Nora, Woodstock, Karl, and Alexis ducked behind a table. Jake peeked out. Mrs. Blunt was sitting opposite the reporter, who was holding his camera up, ready to take a picture of her. Neither of them saw Creature run across the floor toward them.

"Smile!" the reporter was saying.

"I *am* smiling," Mrs. Blunt said, pulling her usual shark-like grimace.

"Um, maybe try a different smile? More, I dunno, *cheerful* . . ."

The reporter's voice trailed off. Jake saw the man's face freeze into an image of absolute horror, as Creature's ketchup-and-fry-covered head slowly rose up over Mrs. Blunt's left shoulder. Creature's eyes were fixed on the large strawberry milkshake that sat on the table in front of Mrs. Blunt.

Mrs. Blunt noticed the reporter's expression of terror.

"My smile isn't that bad —" The words froze on her lips, as a soggy, sticky paw was planted on her shoulder. She turned her head, very, very slowly . . .

"AAAAARGGHHHHHHH!" Mrs. Blunt howled.

"AAARRRRR- AAH- AH- AAH- ARRRRRRRRR!" Creature howled, louder and more Tarzan-like.

Still howling, he vaulted over Mrs. Blunt's shoulder, snatched her milkshake off the table, and made a wild leap straight up toward a ceiling light. He managed to grab the light with one paw, but he couldn't keep the milkshake glass upright.

Jake watched in fascinated horror as the glass tipped further and further over, until the contents of the glass poured in a thick, pink waterfall — SPLOSH! — onto Mrs. Blunt's head.

The reporter stared at Mrs. Blunt. Mrs. Blunt stared at the reporter, a slimy pink

river flowing down her
nose and dripping off
her chin. She wiped
some of it away and
stared at it as though it
was alien snot.

"Eurrrrrgh," she said. Her
eyes glazed over and then she
slowly slumped forward in a
dead faint, directly into the
sticky pool of milkshake on
the table.

The reporter seemed to
finally come to his senses.
He jumped up.

"Stretcher!" he shouted.
"Nurse! Pest control!"

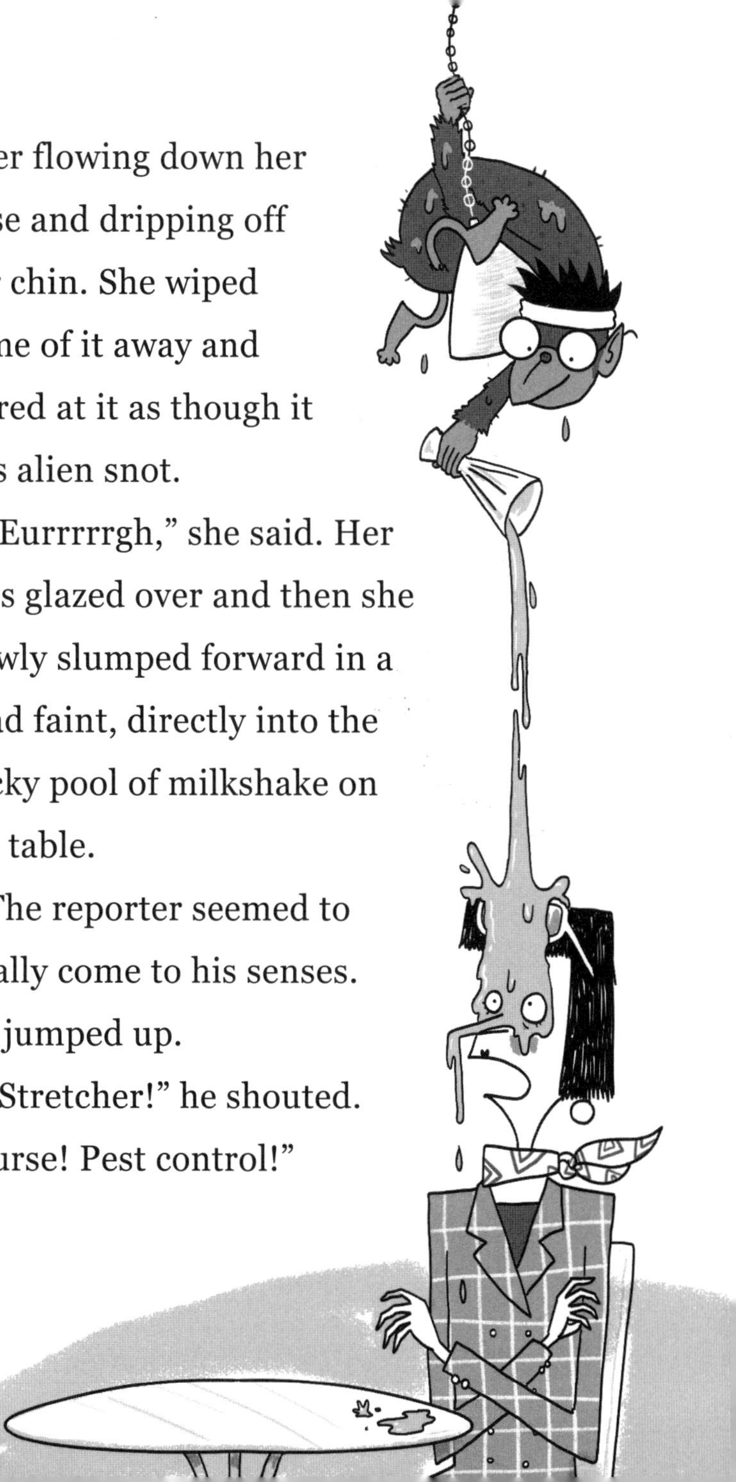

A crowd gathered around Mrs. Blunt, trying to revive her. No one paid any attention to Jake, so he limped back to where the others were hiding behind the table.

"We've got to get Creature out of here," Jake said under his breath.

Nora looked up. "He's gone!"

Jake looked too. All he saw was the light, swinging gently.

"He couldn't have gone far . . ." thought Jake out loud.

Woodstock jumped up. "Everyone, spread out and try to find him!"

"No," said Alexis. She spoke for the first time in ages.

The others looked at her.

"We have got to get ourselves ready for the semi-finals game," she snapped.

"Creature will just have to look after himself this time."

Jake shook his head. "Creature *can't* look after himself! You know what he's like. He'll get in all kinds of trouble."

Nora nodded. "I agree. Getting Mr. Hyde back safe and sound is more important than winning a soccer game."

Alexis put her hands on her hips. "I'm the captain! You have to do what I say!"

"You sounded just like Amelia then," Karl said. Alexis went bright red and opened her mouth to retort.

This is no good, Jake thought. "Guys, stop it! This isn't getting us anywhere."

Suddenly, out of the corner of his eye, Jake saw the vending machine shaking. He nudged Nora.

"What's that machine doing?"

A pair of sticky, furry legs was poking out of the dispenser at the bottom of the machine, thrashing madly.

"It's Creature! He's stuck!" Karl said.

Jake ran over and started pulling Creature's legs.

"Wait, you'll hurt him," Nora said. She hurried over and they gently eased Creature out of the machine. He flailed about like an enraged eel, then went limp.

"He's faking," Karl said, but then there was a loud, snotty snore.

Jake grinned. "He's asleep!"

Woodstock ran over with a tablecloth. "Here . . ."

They wrapped the snoring Creature up in the cloth.

Jake turned to Alexis. "See, he can't look after himself!"

Alexis shrugged. "Well, he's safe now. So let's get on with winning this tournament!"

CHAPTER 6

TEAM MAD AT BANANA JERSEY MIX-UP!

With the sleeping Creature wrapped in the tablecloth, they raced out of the cafeteria into the locker room, just opposite the changing rooms, as a voice came over the loudspeaker.

"FIFTEEN MINUTES TO KICK-OFF!"

"We need to change into the new jerseys," Alexis said, opening the door to the girls' changing room. "Oh, Amelia! What's wrong?"

Amelia was standing there, jersey-bag in hand and a grim look on her face.

"See for yourself!"

Everyone crowded around. Jake hung back — he couldn't let Amelia see Creature. Looking around, he spotted a big locker. *Perfect!* He carefully slid the sleeping Creature into an empty locker and closed the door. When he turned back, Amelia was pulling a yellow jersey out of the bag.

Our jerseys aren't yellow, Jake thought.

"These aren't jerseys!" Alexis cried. "They're banana costumes!"

"Yes," Amelia said. "Who would play such a nasty trick?"

"What makes you think it was on purpose?" Karl asked.

Amelia smirked. "I don't want to blame anyone, but *Barnaby* gave me the bag."

Jake glared at her. "Barnaby wouldn't do that to us!" But as he spoke, a memory popped into his head. *What had Alexis said to Barnaby earlier? "I'd never be seen dead in a banana costume!" And Barnaby was angry about being a banana. Could he have done this to get Alexis back?* Reluctantly, he told the others his suspicions.

Alexis listened and then looked about ready to explode. "You're right, it must have been Barnaby!"

"Let's find him and get the real jerseys back!" Woodstock cried.

Alexis shook her head. "No time. We'll have to wear these."

She disappeared with Amelia into the girls' changing room. Jake, Karl, and Woodstock went into the boys' changing room and pulled on the banana costumes.

They filed back into the locker room.
After a minute, Alexis and Amelia appeared
in full banana suits.

Five bananas looked at each other
silently.

"We look ridiculous," Karl said finally.
"I'm not playing in this."

"Me neither," Woodstock said, slumping down on a bench.

"At least they're the right size," Jake said, trying to lighten the mood. It didn't work. There was another gloomy silence.

Suddenly, Alexis spoke. "Listen, everyone. I don't want to wear a banana costume, either." She raised her voice. "But this isn't about how we look. It's about going onto that field and giving it our all!"

Everyone stared at Alexis. There was fire in her eyes.

"Who cares if people laugh?" she cried. "We will see this to the end! We will play in oversized shirts. We will play in humongous shorts. We will play in banana costumes. We will NEVER SURRENDER!"

Woodstock jumped up. "Yeah!"

"Let's do it!" Karl shouted.

"WHAT ARE WE?" Alexis yelled.

"WINNERS!" they roared back.

"Weirdos, is more like it," Jake heard Amelia mutter from behind him. He turned, but felt a sudden stab of pain in his ankle. Nora looked at him, concerned.

"You can't play with your ankle, Jake!" Jake started to protest, but Alexis nodded. "Nora's right, Jake. We'll bring on Ralph "

"ALL PLAYERS TO THE FIELD!" barked the loudspeaker.

"Woodstock, grab a jersey for Ralph. Time to play ball!"

Alexis marched out, followed by Karl, Woodstock, and Amelia.

The door slammed shut, leaving Nora and Jake alone in the suddenly quiet lobby.

RATTLE.

Nora froze. "What was that?"

RATTLE.

"I don't know," Jake said, looking around.

RAT-AT-AT-AT-AT-AT-AT-AT-ATTLE!

The locker was rocking backward and forward as if alive. Jake jumped up.

"Creature!"

He ran to the locker and opened the door, just in time to catch Creature as he rocketed out. At the same moment, Jake heard voices outside the locker room door.

"Someone is coming!" cried Jake.

"Quick!" Nora disappeared into the girls' changing room. Jake hesitated, but Nora's arm shot back out and yanked him in.

"It's OK," she said, "no one's in here."

In the nick of time! As the door swung closed, Creature squirmed out of Jake's arms, swung around a coat rack three times, and launched himself up to the ceiling. He landed on a beam and perched there, picking fries out of his fur and flinging them down. One landed in Nora's hair.

"Stop it, Creature!" she exclaimed, picking it out. "Oh, why did we let Mr. Hyde get over-excited?"

"Maybe he'd change back if he got really bored," Jake said.

Nora thought. "Well, we could try teaching him the multiplication table. That's pretty boring."

"You're right! Creature — repeat after me. One times two is . . ."

"**Jeeper,**" Creature said.

"No — one times two is two," Nora said, crossly. "Two twos are . . ."

"**Jeeper.**"

"No, four. Three twos are . . ."
"**JEEPPPPPPERRRRRRRRR!**"
Creature started hurling himself frantically around the changing room.

"It's making him worse!" Jake noticed a whiteboard on the wall. "I know, you could do some game tactics stuff on the board. That's pretty bor — um — relaxing."

Nora gave Jake a look, but she picked up the pen and started drawing.

"So, the box formation gives a balance between attack and defense, but if the other team is strong . . ."

Jake glanced at Creature. He was staring, eyes glazed, at Nora's diagram. Maybe it was working!

". . . a pyramid formation would — HEY!"

Creature snatched the pen out of Nora's hand and scribbled "CREECHER ROOLZ" all over her diagram.

Nora grabbed the pen back. "You've spelled that wrong." She started writing it out again, correctly. "C-R-E-A . . ."

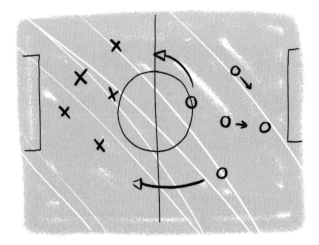

Jake laughed. "Hey, Nora, never mind the spelling —"

HONK! A fart erupted from Creature's bottom. Three seconds later, a hollow ringing sound filled the air. Jake and Nora held their noses. Creature held his too.

"Eurgh!" Jake exclaimed. "That's gross!"

Creature let off a volley of strong, smelly farts, filling the changing room with fumes. Jake nudged Nora.

"Maybe he needs . . ." started Jake.

"A cork?" suggested Nora.

"The bathroom!" Jake said. "Quick, before we're gassed!"

They grabbed Creature and led him to the bathroom. Jake opened the door and slid Creature in. He heard a stall door slam, then what sounded like an underwater volcano erupting.

Then silence.

"He must have finished," Nora said.

Jake opened the stall door. "Creature?"

He walked in and pushed the door to each stall. The end one was locked.

Jake knocked. No answer. Uneasily, Jake knelt down and peered under the door.

Empty.

But a small window, high up in the wall, was wide open.

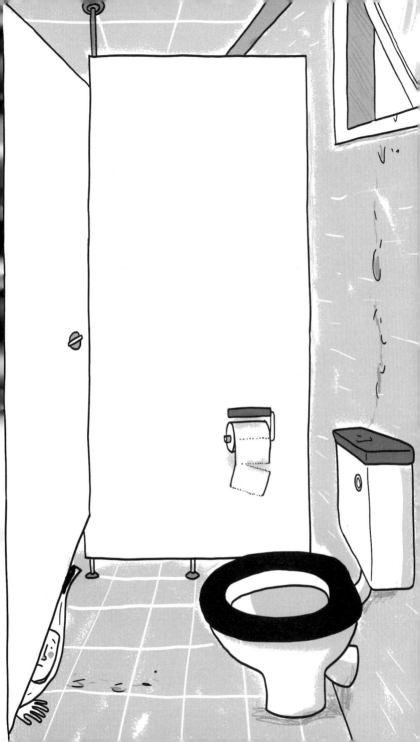

CHAPTER 7

TEAM CAPTAIN MAKES DIFFICULT DECISION

"He's gone!" Jake shouted to Nora.

"No!"

"Yes! Out the window." Jake scrambled to his feet and hobbled back to the door, trying to ignore the pain in his ankle. "Come on, we can't let him escape!"

He followed Nora as she ran across the changing room and out into the locker room. As they reached the main door, it burst open, and Alexis, Karl, and Woodstock ran in, laughing and chattering. Alexis grabbed Jake and started swinging him around.

"WE WON! WE'RE THROUGH TO THE FINAL!" she cheered.

"Ow . . . Alexis . . . stop . . . listen . . .
Creature . . ." Jake gasped as he whirled
around and around.

Alexis let go and twirled Nora instead.

"2−1! What a game!" Woodstock shouted,
doing a victory dance with Karl.

Jake waved his hands. "Guys, listen —"

"That last goal was awesome, Woodstock!" Karl shouted. He started singing.

"Weeeeeeeee are the champions, my frieeeeend . . ."

"PAY ATTENTION TO JAKE!" Nora shouted. Alexis, Karl, and Woodstock stopped leaping about and looked at Jake.

"We need to tell you — hang on." Jake looked around the room. "Where are Amelia and Ralph?"

"Amelia broke a nail and had to be stretchered off," Karl said.

Jake stared. "Really?"

Woodstock giggled. "She wasn't stretchered off, but she made such a fuss you'd think she'd broken a leg. Her mom took her off to get bandaged up. And Ralph went to get a banana smoothie."

"That's good. We don't have much time," Jake said.

Woodstock looked puzzled. "For what?"

"Time to prepare for the next game, of course," Alexis said, jumping up, a crazed look in her eye. "Let's get our game plan together. We're so close to winning! The cup is as good as mine . . . I mean, ours —"

"Actually, that wasn't what I meant," Jake interrupted. "Creature has escaped. We have to go and look for him — now!"

Alexis crossed her arms. "Fine. Go ahead."

"Alexis, we need your help," Nora said. "You play soccer here every week — you're the only one of us who knows her way around."

Jake nodded. Alexis stared at Nora, then at Jake, her cheeks flushed.

"Don't you get it?" she snapped. "This is the most important game of my life! We HAVE to win that trophy! And we won't if we all have to go off on a wild goose chase after that stupid Creature."

She stopped. Everyone stared at her in silence. Nora looked shocked.

"Karl was right. You really are starting to sound like Amelia."

Before Alexis could reply, the door swung open again. A banana-clad head poked around it.

"Oh, here you are —"

"BARNABY MCCRUMB!" Alexis strode forward and dragged him inside.

"What did you do with our jerseys?!" she shouted.

Barnaby stared at Alexis's banana costume. His eyes flicked to Woodstock, Karl, and Jake, in theirs.

"I —"

"You swapped our jerseys for these banana costumes!" Alexis cried.

Barnaby started to open his mouth again.

"And don't you *dare* deny it!"

Barnaby flushed cherry red. "Fine, I won't!"

He turned on his heel and stomped back out of the door. It was only then that Jake noticed a man standing in the doorway. He stepped aside to let Barnaby through.

"Hi kids, hope I'm not interrupting anything," the man said, happily. "I'm Phil, from the *Gazette.*"

Jake recognized him as the reporter they'd seen in the cafeteria with Mrs. Blunt. Amelia was hovering behind him.

"I just want a little interview with the captain, if she's around," Phil said.

Alexis took a few deep breaths. She stepped forward and showed her captain's armband proudly.

"I'm Alexis. I'm the captain."

Amelia pushed past the reporter to stand next to Alexis. "And I'm the vice-captain," she said loudly.

The reporter glanced at her. "Oh, hello." He turned back to Alexis and held out a microphone.

"So, Alexis, how confident are you of winning today?"

"Well, Phil," Alexis said, "we've been training very hard —"

Suddenly, Amelia thrust her face at the microphone. "Very confident," she said. "With me on the field, we're bound to win! I wore out the other team in our last game. Did you see it?"

The reporter looked at her. "Sorry, no, I didn't. What do you think, Alexis?"

"Our game plan is strong, thanks to —"

"Thanks to me, we won the last two games!" Amelia interrupted. "I set up those two goals single-handedly! I'm a natural soccer player. Just ask Daddy . . ."

"Actually, that's not —" Alexis began, but Amelia grabbed the microphone from the reporter and turned so that Alexis couldn't reach it.

"You know, Daddy is one of the sponsors today. He owns Burt's Banana Smoothies. But anyway, let's talk about me."

Alexis tried again. "It's working as a team that's important —"

But Amelia butted in again. "Personality is the most important thing. The cup is as good as mine . . . I mean ours —"

Alexis made a strange noise in her throat. Jake looked at her. She was staring at Amelia as though she'd seen a ghost. It hit Jake why — Alexis had said exactly the same words a few minutes before!

Jake heard Amelia declaring, "It's all about winning . . ."

"ENOUGH! That's it!" A pale-faced Alexis ripped off her captain's armband. Everyone stared at her. The reporter raised his eyebrows and scribbled something in his notebook.

"What are you doing?" Woodstock asked, astonished.

Alexis looked at Amelia. "It's not *all* about winning. Winning is great, but —" she looked over at Nora and Jake — "supporting your friends and being there for them is more important."

She swallowed hard and held the armband out to Amelia. "If you want to win so much — here, have this. I resign the captaincy. You're the captain now, Amelia."

CHAPTER 8

COMMENTATOR ATTACKED BY GIANT BANANAS!

A triumphant look crept over Amelia's face. She grabbed the armband from Alexis and put it on, just as an announcement came over the loudspeaker — the final game was about to start!

"Right, we've got a game to win!" Amelia turned to the confused reporter. "I'm captain now, so you'll want some photos of me," she said, taking his arm and dragging him out of the locker room. "Make sure you get my best side . . ."

"Karl, Woodstock — you'd better go too," Alexis said, as Amelia and the reporter disappeared.

"Aren't you going to play at all, then?" Woodstock asked.

Alexis shook her head. "Like you guys said: I have to help look for Creature. You'll need to take a jersey for Oliver."

She gave Karl the last banana costume, and he and Woodstock reluctantly trooped off. Alexis watched them go, then heaved a big sigh. Nora put an arm around her shoulders.

"Alexis, you didn't have to —"

"I did. I *was* starting to sound like Amelia. I'm not really like her, am I?"

Jake shook his head. "No. You just proved that."

Alexis stood tall.

"Well, we can't hang around — we've got a Creature to catch!"

Jake slapped his forehead. "Of course! Come on . . ."

Outside, the crowd was moving as one toward the main field, ready for the final game. Dotted around in the crowd, Jake could see the bobbing tops of the student council's banana costumes, and a band was playing. It was like being at a carnival.

Nora made a face. "How will we find him in this crowd?"

"It shouldn't be hard," Jake said. "He usually leaves a trail of chaos behind him."

As they peered around, trying to spot a trail of chaos, a nearby loudspeaker crackled on. Jake was expecting a "five minutes to kick off" type announcement. So he was very surprised to hear a familiar voice sing out . . .

"JEEP-JEEP-JEEPERRRR!"

Nora, Jake, and Alexis stared at each other.

"Creature!" Jake grabbed Alexis. "He must be in the commentator's box! Do you know where it is?"

"It's at the other end of the main field! Come on!"

Alexis started running, followed by Nora. Still limping, Jake tried to keep them in sight as they dodged through the crowds lining the fields.

"JEEP-JEEP-JEEPPERRRR!" came Creature's voice again over the loudspeaker. Jake could see people in the crowd looking at each other in confusion.

"Maybe *Jeeper* is the other team's nickname?" he heard someone say.

"No, they're the Bananas! Hello, here's an escaped banana!"

Jake felt his face burning as people laughed and pointed at him, but he said nothing and limped on. As the whistle blew for kick-off, a chant went around their team's supporters.

"COME ON, YOU BANANAS!"

Ahead, Alexis was beckoning urgently. "Jake! Up here . . ."

A flight of steps led up to a low building with glass windows along the front. As they reached the top of the steps, Jake saw a short, black-haired man outside, banging furiously on the door. His face was blown up like an angry puffer fish, and he was holding a large strawberry milkshake in one hand.

"Some joker's locked me out!" he burst out. "And now they're making silly noises into the microphone. Everyone will think it's me!" He hammered on the door again.

"Let me in, you loony, or I'm calling the police!"

"BU-U-U-UUUUUUUUURRR RRRRRRRRR-R-R-R-R-R-P!"

One of Creature's impressively long burps echoed around the soccer complex. Jake saw the sea of heads below him turn to look up at the commentator's box. He pulled Alexis and Nora to one side.

"What now?" he muttered.

"There's usually a window open around the back," Alexis whispered. "Follow me."

Leaving the commentator banging on the door, Jake and Nora followed Alexis to the rear of the building. Sure enough, a window was open, just big enough to climb through. Jake gave Alexis a leg-up. She was having difficulty as her banana costume caught on the window latch, but she made it. Amelia

grabbed Jake's hand and yanked him up.

"Ouch! It's my ankle . . ."

"Sorry!"

Jake eased himself through, trying not to bash his sore ankle on the window. "Stupid banana costumes!" he said, as his suit also caught on the window latch. "We should have taken them off . . ."

He finally unhooked himself and lowered

himself down into a small kitchen area, with a door on the other side. As Alexis pulled Nora through the window, Jake tiptoed over to the door and turned the handle.

Squeeeeeeee-e-e-eak!

"Jake!" Alexis said. "Creature will hear! I'll do it . . ."

Alexis carefully turned the handle and pushed the door open a crack.

"I think I can see him," she whispered.

Jake peeked through. He saw a long desk in front of the big windows that looked out onto the fields. In front of this was a large leather swivel chair. It was facing away from him but over the chair back, he could see Creature's scruffy pile of dark hair.

"I'll go this side, Jake — you go the other," Alexis whispered. "Nora, get ready to grab him if he manages to escape."

Quiet as mice, they tiptoed toward the chair. Closer . . . closer . . .

"GOTCHA!" Alexis shouted. As she hurled herself around the chair and grabbed Creature, Jake did the same on his side.

There was a terrified howl. But it wasn't a Creature howl.

It wasn't Creature's patch of black hair they'd seen over the chair back.

It was the commentator's!

Jake and Alexis jumped back as if they'd been burned. Nora was still behind the chair and couldn't see anything.

"What's the matter?!" she cried.

Before anyone could say or do anything,
the commentator grabbed the microphone.

"MURDER! ROBBERY! I'M BEING
ATTACKED BY GIANT BANANAS!"

CHAPTER 9

TEAM CAPTAIN CAUSES A RUCKUS WITH REF!

"MURDER! ROBBERY! I'M BEING ATTACKED BY GIANT BANANAS!" The commentator's words reverberated around the grounds.

Out of the window, Jake saw a sea of startled faces below swivel to look up at the commentator's box. Some people even started to run toward it.

Jake's brain went into overdrive. He grabbed the microphone from the gibbering commentator and spoke in the deepest voice he could muster.

"I MEAN THE . . . THE BANANAS ARE REALLY MURDERING THE OPPOSITION . . . UM, IT'S LIKE

DAYLIGHT ROBBERY . . . AND I'M REALLY ADMIRING THE ATTACKING TACTICS OF THE BANANAS TODAY!"

It was strange to hear his voice ringing out across the stadium, ten times louder than it usually was! Jake breathed a huge sigh of relief as the crowd slowly turned their faces from the commentator's box back to the game.

"Give me that!" The commentator seized the microphone from Jake. "What are you kids doing? Nearly gave me a heart attack!"

"We're really sorry," Alexis said. "We were trying to catch that, joker — the one who locked you out. Where is he?"

The commentator pointed to the door.

"He left, but only after burping in my face, knocking my milkshake over, and then running off between my legs! A kid dressed as a monkey — what's next? And you kids are dressed as bananas. It's madness!" The man glared at Jake. "So he's in your gang, huh? I'm going to report this." He grabbed a pen and notebook. "What are your names?"

Alexis gave Jake a scared look.

"I haven't got all day! What's your name, boy?"

Not knowing what else to do, Jake opened his mouth to speak, when Nora gave a cry.

"Something's happening on the field!"

The commentator whipped around. Jake and Alexis ran to the window.

Down on the field, Jake could see Amelia yelling at the referee, while the rest of the players crowded around, waving their arms.

The commentator grabbed the microphone and started talking very fast into it.

"WELL, LOOKS LIKE THE REF AWARDED A FREE KICK JUST OUTSIDE THE BOX, BUT THERE'S SOME KIND OF DISPUTE OVER WHO'S GOING TO TAKE IT. THE CAPTAIN OF THE BANANAS IS

GOING BANANAS! WHO KNOWS WHAT SHE
JUST SAID TO THE REF . . ."

"Amelia's causing trouble," Alexis said. "She'll get sent off if she's not careful. We can't afford to lose a player now!"

"SHE'LL BE CARDED, FOR SURE."

The ref pulled out a yellow card and held it up to Amelia.

"YELLOW CARD! LOOKS AS IF THE
CAPTAIN'S GOING TO APPEAL . . .
BUT NO, WHAT'S HAPPENING NOW?
SHE'S RUNNING BACK TO THE BALL,
AND — OH DEAR! — SHE'S KICKED THE
BALL AWAY. A CASE OF SOUR GRAPES,
I THINK . . ."

Open-mouthed, Jake, Alexis, and Nora watched as the red-faced Amelia whacked the ball as hard as she could toward the goal. But she sliced it, and, instead of

rocketing straight into the
net, it soared off toward the
sideline in a graceful curve.

"THERE'S A BANANA
KICK IF EVER I SAW
ONE!" the commentator cried.

"Tsk," Nora tutted. "Terrible angle!"

The ball flew toward the crowd.

Jake stared. "It's going to hit
someoooooooooooone . . ."

THWACK!

It hit a tall woman smack on the back of the head. Even from a distance, Jake could see who it was. There was no mistaking that black, sharply bobbed hair, although it was looking slightly pinker than usual after the strawberry milkshake accident.

"Mrs. Blunt!" Alexis said, covering her mouth.

"Ooh, I can't look," Nora said, but she did.

Mrs. Blunt staggered, flailed her arms around, then sank in a heap on the ground.

From up in the box, Jake saw the crowd go completely still.

But only for a second. Jake couldn't hear much, but he saw people waving and their mouths opening and closing, as if he was watching TV with the sound turned down. A first-aid team raced up and disappeared into the crowd. A minute later they emerged, with Mrs. Blunt on a stretcher.

Jake felt a nudge in his ribs.

"Let's go," Nora said, quietly. "Before *he* notices."

She rolled her eyes toward the commentator, who was still speaking at top speed. He seemed to have forgotten about Jake, Alexis, and Nora, who tiptoed out quietly. As the door closed behind him, Jake felt something sticky underfoot.

"Ugh, what's that?!" he exclaimed, looking down. He'd stepped in a puddle of gooey pink stuff.

"Milkshake!" Nora said. "I stepped in it too. Creature spilled it, didn't he?"

"Look!" Alexis pointed. Leading away from the puddle of milkshake at the door was a trail of strawberry pink paw prints.

Jake laughed. "Creature got covered in milkshake — again! This should be easy."

They followed the paw prints down the steps, then back past the fields toward the locker room. The prints got fainter and fainter. Finally, they disappeared.

Alexis scratched her head. "Which way now?"

They were standing next to a small white tent with a red cross on it. Inside, Jake could hear someone talking in a loud voice.

"It's very white in here. Is this the White House? You must be the President. Wonderful to meet you, Your Presidentness!"

"That's Mrs. Blunt!" Nora said. "What's she mumbling on about?"

All three crept to the opening of the tent and listened.

"You're very small. I always thought the President would be bigger!"

Jake suppressed a snort of laughter. "That knock sent her silly in the head," he whispered to Nora and Alexis.

Mrs. Blunt's voice was getting more and more muffled for some reason.

"I must say, you have extremely hairy hands, Mr. President."

Jake, Alexis, and Nora stared at each other.

"Could it — no, there's no way it could possibly be . . ."

CHAPTER 10

PRINCIPAL'S BRAINS ALTERED AFTER ALIEN ABDUCTION

"Hairy hands?" Nora breathed in Jake's ear. "You don't think . . ."

Jake peered through the tent flap, then jerked back in shock.

An Egyptian mummy was looking silently at him.

Jake took a deep breath, then peeked again.

He breathed out. Egyptian mummies didn't wear high heels. It was Mrs. Blunt. And she wasn't looking at him. In fact, she couldn't see him at all because her head was completely wrapped in bandages.

On a trolley next to her sat a box from which a scuffling noise was coming. Then Creature's head popped out of it. He was winding a bandage around Mrs. Blunt's head. He'd already wrapped her arms and torso.

As Jake watched, Creature got himself in a knot with the bandages. He turned around and around, getting more and more tangled up. Then, with a yelp, he fell off the trolley, pulling the box of bandages down on top of himself.

"Neeeeep!"

"Ooommmfff?" Mrs. Blunt mumbled through the bandages.

"Where are the medical personnel?" Jake heard Nora whisper from behind him. "Gone to deal with another injury, probably," he whispered back.

Glancing around to make sure no one was coming, he pushed the tent flap back and tiptoed inside.

"What are you doing?!" Alexis cried.

"Getting Creature!" Jake skirted past the mummified Mrs. Blunt, who was frantically trying to yank her arms free.

"Oomffa-oomffa-OOMFF!" Mrs. Blunt staggered to her feet, as Jake hurled himself at the upside-down bandage box . . .

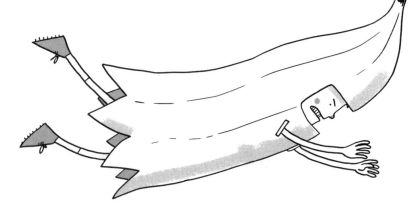

. . . and missed.

Jake caught a glimpse of Creature's eyes through a slit in the box, before it bolted toward the tent door, a trail of bandages billowing out behind it.

"OOOMFFFA-OOOMFFFA-OOOMFFF!" Mrs. Blunt's "oomffs" were getting more panicked.

"Stop that box!" Jake shouted, seeing Nora and Alexis's faces staring through the tent flap. Nora grabbed for it, but the box veered the other way.

CR-R-R-RASH!! It crashed into a trolley piled with medical supplies. The

trolley fell over in an avalanche of boxes and bottles. Creature's box shot out from under the trolley, straight into Mrs. Blunt's legs.

"Ooooomfffff!" Mrs. Blunt oomffed again. The box ran in circles around her legs, wrapping them in trailing bandages, with Jake close behind. Mrs. Blunt tried to step forward. But her ankles were now tightly bound. She tripped and toppled . . .

"Got you!" Alexis and Nora ran forward and caught the falling principal, as Jake flung himself on top of the runaway box.

"Eeeee! Eeeee!" The box shook Jake till his teeth rattled. Finally it went still.

Jake peeked cautiously through the slit. Inside, Creature was slumped, panting. He looked thoroughly pooped.

Nora and Alexis unwound Mrs. Blunt, from the toes up. Finally, her eyes appeared, blinking in the light. Her voice wobbled a bit as she spoke.

"Why it's Nora, isn't it? And, let me see, Alexis and Jake! Thank you for rescuing me, my dear children."

Alexis, Nora, and Jake looked at each other, at a loss for words. What had got into Mrs. Blunt? She never had a nice word to say to anyone!

There was a rustle at the tent door.

"How are you doing — hey, what's going on here?"

A white-coated woman was standing in the doorway, looking at them in surprise.

Mrs. Blunt stepped forward. "Let me explain, doctor. I was just lying on the couch here, having a nice chat with the President of the United States, when aliens came down and wrapped me in some kind of cocoon."

The woman clucked her tongue.

"I think you'd better lie down," she said. "You must have a concussion! Let me see that bump." She led the principal back to the couch. "And you kids, get going now, please!"

Grabbing the box with Creature in, Jake ducked out of the tent. As Nora and Alexis appeared behind him, a shrill whistle blew over at the main field.

"It's half-time," Alexis said. "Shall we go and see what's happening? And then take Creature back to the changing rooms?"

Jake peeked into the box. "He's asleep. OK, but we'll have to be quick."

As they approached the field, Jake saw a bunch of sad-looking bananas trudging glumly off. To his surprise, he saw that there were only three players — Amelia, Woodstock, and the last substitute, Oliver.

Amelia threw herself on the ground dramatically.

"It's hopeless!" she wailed, wiping a muddy hand across her muddy face and making it even muddier. "We're losing 7–0!"

"7–0?" Alexis cried. "How come? And where are Karl and Ralph?"

"Amelia kept yelling at Karl," Woodstock said, angrily. "So he stomped off, saying he'd rather practice the band's award-ceremony routine. Then Ralph got poked in the eye so he left too. Two of you will have to come back and play."

"What's the point?! We'll never win," Amelia wailed from the ground. "I don't want to be captain any more!" She crawled over and clutched Alexis's leg. "Please, be captain again! I'm not a natural soccer player, I'm much better at pony riding."

Alexis patted Amelia's head awkwardly.

"You'll be fine, Amelia! You're a strong person, you can do this —"

Amelia looked up at Alexis. Her lip wobbled. Then her face crumpled and she burst into a long wailing sob.

"Waaaaaaaaaaaaaaaaaah!"

The box in Jake's arms twitched. Jake held it tighter and looked nervously through the slit, but Creature's eyes were still closed.

"I'm not a strong person," Amelia howled. "I'm a horrible person!"

Alexis rolled her eyes. "You haven't been that bad, Amelia . . ."

Amelia scrambled to her feet, smearing mud and tears all over her face. She grabbed Alexis by the shoulders.

"You don't understand." She stared around at everyone. "I've done something terrible!"

There was a confused silence.

"What have you done, Amelia?" Nora finally asked.

Amelia swallowed hard.

"It wasn't Barnaby who swapped the jerseys for banana costumes. It was me."

CHAPTER 11

NEWS OF FOUL PLAY SHOCKS TEAM

"*You?* It was you who swapped our jerseys for banana costumes?" Alexis said, a stunned look on her face.

Amelia hung her head. "Yes."

There was a short, shocked silence. Jake's mind whirled. But that was impossible! *Why, he'd watched Barnaby give the bag to Amelia himself. But then she'd been in the changing room on her own; she would have had time . . .* It still didn't make sense.

"But why?" he asked. "You knew you'd have to wear one yourself!"

Amelia stared at the ground. "I-I-I thought Alexis would refuse to play wearing one. Because of what she said earlier — that she wouldn't be seen dead in a banana costume."

Jake felt a sudden hot flush of guilt. *What an idiot I am!* Amelia had heard that comment, too, not just Barnaby. How could he have suspected Barnaby, and not Amelia?! And he had caused the others to think . . .

He opened his mouth, but Nora got there before him.

"You did it so you could be captain! Did you lock Alexis in the bathroom too?"

Amelia nodded, biting her lip.

"I don't care much for soccer," she sniffed. "But I did want to be captain. So I asked Daddy to get me on the team. He'd just made a big donation to Mrs. Blunt's Principal Statue Fund, so he had a word with Mrs. Blunt yesterday and she put me on the team. But she wouldn't make me captain!"

Jake couldn't bear it any longer. He burst out. "The worst thing is that you made us blame Barnaby."

"Blame me for what?"

Jake turned. Barnaby was standing behind him, still in his banana costume and looking extremely fed up.

"Tell him, Amelia," Jake said.

Amelia spoke with an effort. "I-I-I swapped the jerseys. After you gave me the bag, I swapped the jerseys for banana costumes. But I made them think you did it." She paused and cleared her throat. "I'm, well, I'm — sorrrr-aargh." She sort of gurgled the last word.

Barnaby stared at her. "What?"

"Sorrr-reurgh."

Barnaby shook his head. "Still not sure what you're saying . . ."

"SORRY!" Amelia finally spat the word out. Jake thought she'd probably never said it in her life before.

"Apology accepted." Barnaby grinned. "It was quite funny. Wish I'd thought of it."

"Barnaby!" Nora said, shocked.

Jake shook his head. "But Barnaby, why didn't you say anything when we accused you of swapping the jerseys? Why didn't you say it wasn't you?"

Barnaby shrugged.

"You guys always think I'm up to no good. Everyone thinks that. You'd made up your minds it was me; you'd never have believed me if I'd said it wasn't."

"That's not true —" Woodstock began.

Barnaby stopped him. "It *is* true. Plus, I was in a bad mood. I really wanted to play today! I'm not very good at much, but I'm pretty good at soccer. Finally, I had the chance to prove I could do something well for a change. And instead I had to wander around dressed as a banana, helping old people to their seats."

"Well, we all ended up as bananas," Woodstock said, "and you were good at showing people to their seats. My granddad seems to like you." He pointed. Jake looked along the sideline to see Woodstock's granddad waving his megaphone.

"HELLO BANANABY!" he roared.

Barnaby winced. "Great, I make a good banana. And old people like me."

"It's good to be liked," Nora said.

"Anyway, you're good at a lot of stuff," Jake said. "Like when you make rhythms with your mouth . . ."

"Beatboxing." A slight smile twitched on Barnaby's mouth. "Yeah, s'pose I am."

"You're a great friend," Woodstock said.

"And . . ." Alexis leaned forward and whispered so that Amelia wouldn't hear, "you're really good with Creature." She turned to the others. "I think we should all apologize to Barnaby for suspecting him of swapping the jerseys."

They all nodded. "Sorry, Barnaby," everyone said.

Just then the loudspeaker burst into life.

"FIVE MINUTES TO THE SECOND HALF! TEAMS, PREPARE FOR THE FINAL SHOWDOWN!"

Amelia looked pleadingly at Alexis. "Please go on instead of me," she begged. "If you go do, we might have a chance!"

Woodstock looked at Amelia in disgust. "Amelia, you're being a scaredy-cat. I bet you just don't want to be on the field when we lose! Then you can tell everyone it wasn't your fault. Maybe we should tell Mrs. Blunt what you did."

Amelia went pale. Alexis shook her head. "I don't think so, Woodstock. She's learned her lesson. Haven't you, Amelia?"

Amelia nodded eagerly. "Oh yes, I have! I won't do it again, honest! Please don't tell Mrs. Blunt. I'll do anything . . ."

Alexis raised her eyebrows. "Anything?"

"Anything," Amelia repeated.

Alexis planted her hands on her hips. "OK. Get back out there and play some top-quality soccer, then."

Amelia's face fell.

"As goalie," Alexis added.

Amelia's face fell even further. Jake grinned. Playing goalie was not exactly what you wanted to do when the other team was up 7–0.

"OK, team. I'll come on as captain," Alexis said. "But we're two players down. We need one more. Jake, how's your ankle? Do you think you can play?"

Holding the box with Creature tightly, Jake wiggled his ankle. It wasn't as bad as before, but it looked swollen.

"I think I could . . ."

"How about Barnaby?" Nora said suddenly.

Everyone looked at Barnaby. His face lit up. "Really?"

Alexis shrugged. "Why not? The only reason you weren't picked was because you weren't there."

Barnaby punched the air. "Let me at 'em! They don't call me Barnaby Beckham Ronaldo McRooney for nothing!"

Jake laughed. "They don't call you that at all!"

"OK, gang, gather round," Alexis said. "So the team is as follows: me and Barnaby as forward; Amelia as goalie; Woodstock, you and Oliver on defense — Amelia will need as much support as she can get. But keep an eye out for offensive opportunities. We need to get goals and plenty of them! As Mr. Hyde says, WHAT ARE WE?"

"WINNERS!" everyone shouted except Amelia.

"What are we, Amelia?" Alexis said, firmly.

Amelia gulped. "Winners."

CHAPTER 12

GOLDEN BALL TROPHY STOLEN!

The referee was calling the teams back onto the field.

"Here goes," Alexis said. "Are we ready?"

Everyone nodded as the other team appeared. The captain walked up to Alexis, looked her up and down, and laughed.

"Bananas, prepare to be smashed."

"And made into banana cream pie," said another opposing player.

"Banana splits," said another, and they all grabbed their sides laughing. Jake saw Alexis's fists clench and he nudged her.

"Don't let them get to you," he muttered. "Remember what you said earlier — who cares if they laugh?"

Alexis breathed out slowly. "Yeah. They think we're an easy win. We'll show them!"

Nora and Jake shouted encouragement as Alexis, Woodstock, Oliver, Barnaby, and Amelia walked out onto the field. Suddenly Alexis turned and pointed excitedly toward the end of the field. Jake looked, and saw that a platform had been set up. On top sat a gleaming gold trophy in the shape of a soccer ball. The Golden Ball trophy!

Jake tried to give Alexis a thumbs-up, but it was hard with the box in his arms. He peeked through the slit and saw Creature sniffing a bit in his sleep. Nora looked at the box nervously.

"Shouldn't we take him back to the changing rooms?" she asked.

"He's still asleep. Let's watch a few minutes of the game first."

The crowd fell silent. Then . . .

Pheeeeeeeeeeeeeeeep!

"COME ON, YOU BANANAS!"

Jake and Nora both jumped and turned. Woodstock's granddad was sitting in a chair behind them with his megaphone, straining to see over their heads.

"I can't see," Granddad said. "Do you think you could move me forward a little? I'd do it myself, but my hip's no good . . ."

"OK." Jake put the box on the ground and took hold of the chair on one side. Nora took the other. "One, two, three — GO!"

They heaved the chair forward.

"A teensy bit further . . . just a wee bit more . . . nearly there . . ."

Bit by bit, they edged the chair forward. Finally, Granddad was happy.

"Thank you, my dears." Then he bellowed through the megaphone, "COME ON, YOU BANANAS!"

"At least there's nothing wrong with his voice," Nora whispered to Jake.

Jake grinned and leaned forward to try to see what was happening on the field. He saw Alexis take a shot but miss. A striker from the other team moved the ball back up the field. The banana-defenders had all gone forward. This was a dangerous situation!

"Get ready, Amelia!" Jake yelled to Amelia, whose knees were knocking as the striker sprinted toward her.

Nora groaned. "She'll never save it . . ."

But then, without warning, the striker stumbled. The ball rolled harmlessly toward the goal, to be grabbed by a surprised Amelia, as the striker stood completely still, staring at the goal.

"Why has he stopped?" Nora exclaimed.

Jake's eyes moved toward the goal, and then nearly popped out of his head. He grabbed Nora. "Look!"

On top of the goalposts sat Creature, and he held something in his hand. Jake couldn't see what it was, but it glinted in the sunlight.

"How did he get there?" Nora gasped.

Jake slapped his head. "He must have escaped when we were moving Woodstock's granddad's chair!"

An important-looking man in a gray suit burst out of the crowd, not far from Jake.

"Hey! That mascot has snatched the Golden Ball trophy!" he boomed. "Someone call the police!"

Jake stared. It was true — the shiny thing raised above Creature's head was the Golden Ball trophy! Jake groaned. *This is really not what we need,* he thought. He tried to see what was happening, but it was difficult. A crowd of players had gathered around the goal, and officials were running onto the field. He felt Nora grab his arm.

"What's Amelia doing?!" she exclaimed.

Amelia burst out of the little huddle of players and started running up the field with the ball toward the opposite goal, now goalie-free. She reached the box, swung her leg back, and kicked as hard as she could. The ball rocketed into the net. Woodstock's granddad leapt out of his chair as though he'd been shot out of a cannon.

"GOOOOOOOOOOOOOAAAAAAAAAAAL!" he roared, hurting Jake's ears.

The noise startled Creature too. He teetered wildly on the crossbar for a few seconds, still clutching the trophy, then fell off — **POLOLLOP!** — straight into a muddy puddle.

Several players tried to leap on him, but he was covered in mud and slipped through their fingers. He dashed along the goal line, still holding the now very muddy Golden Ball trophy. As he ran past a hot dog stand, a man in a chef's hat and apron ran out, waving a spatula.

"Hey! That's the prankster who did a dive-bomb into my ketchup!"

The man ran after Creature. Two banana-clad student council members joined him. Jake saw that they were carrying a large net, and a horrible vision of a terrified Creature in a cage came to his mind.

"We can't let them catch Creature," he said to Nora. "They'll find out he's not a kid at all. And then who knows what they'll do to him!"

Nora pointed. "He's coming this way. Let's try and grab him!"

Creature had swerved around the corner and was bolting down the sideline toward them. On the field, the game was back in full swing. Jake heard a roar from the crowd, but he had to focus on catching Creature.

Creature got nearer . . . and nearer. Jake prepared to pounce . . .

Just down the sideline, the important-looking man who had wanted to call the police jumped out in front of Creature. At the same moment, the two council members skidded up with their net.

"GOTCHA!" They hurled the net at Creature.

"Nooo!" Jake and Nora cried, together.

CHAPTER 13

THEY THINK IT'S ALL OVER . . .

As if in slow motion, the net came down.

But the student bananas had not planned on anyone but Creature being under it.

"AAARRRGHHH!"

The net fell over the important-looking man, trapping him.

"WAARRGHHH!"

Unable to stop, the hot dog-stand man slammed into the student council bananas, who fell on top of the net. As they all lay there thrashing and yelling, Jake saw Creature's face appear at the bottom of the pile-up. With a wiggle, he squirmed out from under the net and sped off, jeepering triumphantly.

Jake was ready. Quick as lightning, he held out the open box, and Creature hurtled straight into it. He slammed the lid shut just as the final whistle blew.

Pheeeeeeeeeeeeeeep!

"It's a tie!" Nora cried.

Jake stared at the scoreboard. "7–7? How . . . ?"

"JAKE!" Alexis came panting up. "It's a golden goal knockout! The first team to score wins! But Oliver's injured. You'll have to come back on."

Jake shoved the box at Nora.

"Take this." He ran onto the field.

"But your ankle —" Nora shouted.

"It's fine, just look after Creature!" He reached Alexis. "How did we get seven goals?" he asked.

Alexis shrugged. "I guess they thought we'd never catch up, so they didn't even start trying till the last five minutes. Plus we played really well! Now, let's talk tactics."

She called everyone to a huddle.

"We need to work as a team — pass the ball, don't hold on to it, and focus on getting that golden goal!"

"Teams to positions!" The ref put the whistle to his lips.

Pheeeeeeeeeeeeeeeeep!

No sooner had the whistle blown than Alexis passed the ball to Jake. He caught it on his foot, and ran toward the goal. Too late, he spotted a defender coming up. The player hooked the ball from Jake and whacked it back up the field to one of his teammates, right in front of the goal!

THWACK!

"Nooo!" In horror, Jake watched the ball curve toward the goal — but at the last second, Amelia made a superhuman leap and punched the ball away.

Woodstock cheered. "Great save!"

"Play on," the ref said. Alexis got the ball and crossed it to Woodstock, who passed to Jake. Jake dribbled past a defender, and crossed it back to Alexis. Barnaby hovered outside the goal box as Alexis thundered up the field. The goalie crouched, ready. Jake knew Alexis wanted to take the shot, but two defenders were quickly closing in.

"Barnaby!" Alexis shouted. She volleyed the ball toward the far corner of the goal.

The goalie dived. But as the ball sailed past Barnaby, he took a leap and headed it into the opposite corner of the net.

"GOOOOOOOAAAAAAAL!" roared the crowd. Barnaby had scored the golden goal! He sank to his knees.

"We did it — oommmff!"

Jake, Alexis, Amelia, and Woodstock surrounded Barnaby, hoisted him onto their shoulders, and carried him on a victory lap around the field. As they came to where Nora was standing, Woodstock's granddad bellowed into his megaphone.

"WEEEEEE ARE THE CHAMPIONS . . ."

"You were awesome!" Nora shouted.

"Thanks!" Jake grinned, then looked around. "Nora—where's the box?"

"I gave it to Woodstock's granddad —"

Nora's hand flew to her mouth. "Noooo . . ."

Jake looked at Granddad. The box was still on his lap — so why was Nora scared?

Then he realized.

An orange glow was coming from inside the box. It got brighter and brighter. Amelia's mouth dropped open.

"THAT BOX IS ON FIRE!" she shouted.

Too late, Jake hurled himself at the box.

ᶠAAAAAAAAAAAAARRRRRT!

Wheeeeeeee · · · · · · · · · ·

POP! POP! POP!

BANG!

Everyone dived for cover as a cloud of purple smoke erupted around them. Jake heard shouts and could barely see Granddad through the fog. Granddad was still in his chair, flapping his arms and coughing wildly.

But it wasn't just Granddad . . . Jake wafted smoke away.

"Mr. Hyde!" Jake called.

A slightly steaming Mr. Hyde was sitting on Granddad's lap, looking extremely surprised. Granddad looked dazed. Then his eyes lit up, and he grabbed Mr. Hyde by the wrists.

"You must be a genie," he exclaimed. "Can you grant me a wish?"

"I'm sorry, sir, but I'm not a genie," Mr. Hyde said, trying to release himself from Granddad's grip.

"Granddad, this is our teacher. His name is Mr. Hyde," Woodstock said. "Please let him go."

Reluctantly Granddad loosened his grip, and Mr. Hyde stood up quickly.

Amelia crawled out from under a chair and looked around. She stared at Mr. Hyde, a puzzled frown on her face.

"How . . . what . . . why . . . ?"

"Just one of Granddad's smoke bombs," Woodstock said quickly. "Look, your parents are over there, Amelia. They probably want another photograph . . ."

With one last confused look at Mr. Hyde, Amelia ran off, nearly bumping into a crowd of student council bananas who were marching toward the platform.

In the lead was the important-looking man who had been trapped under the net. He was clutching the rather muddy Golden Ball trophy to his chest as if he thought it might vanish at any moment.

Jake realized with a shock of excitement that the trophy now belonged to them! In ten minutes' time, they'd be standing on that platform.

Alexis tugged at Mr. Hyde's sleeve.

"Sir, we won!" she said. "Did you see Barnaby's amazing goal?"

"How could he? He was in the box," Barnaby said. Mr. Hyde patted Barnaby on the back.

"Actually, I did — through the slit," he said. "It was great seeing you guys doing some great teamwork out there. And when Barnaby scored, I thought I would explode from pride."

"And then you did!" Nora laughed.

Mr. Hyde grinned. "Yes, I suppose I did, didn't I?" He scratched his head. "I do have one question, though. Why on earth are you all dressed as bananas?"

"It's a long story," Jake said. "But after you changed into Creature, everything sort of went a little . . . a little . . ."

"Pear-shaped?" Mr. Hyde asked.

Jake, Alexis, Barnaby, Nora, and Woodstock all spoke at the same time.

"BANANAS!"

ABOUT THE AUTHOR

Sam Watkins voraciously consumed books from a young age, due to a food shortage in the village where she grew up. This diet, although not recommended by doctors, has given her a lifelong passion for books. She has been a bookseller, editor, and publisher, and writes and illustrates her own children's books. At one point, things all got a bit too bookish so she decided to be an art teacher for a while, but books won the day in the end.

ABOUT THE ILLUSTRATOR

David O'Connell is an illustrator who lives in London, England. His favorite things to draw are monsters, naughty children (another type of monster), batty old ladies, and evil cats . . . Oh, and teachers that transform into naughty little creatures!